I'm **Atlas**! I'll be your tourguide to the world today. You are in good hands, reader; my resume includes many centuries holding the earth and observing humans throughout the ages. I'm also the title characer of one of the best selling page turners of all time: a book of maps called an "**Atlas**."

To **humans**, the world seems like a very large and scary place, unless they can gather together for barbecues and birthday parties and stuff like that. To do this, they form great nations and cities. Even the **Gods** respect the power of important cities, for--like them--they can be immortal.

Before the **Rock n' Roll Hall of Fame**, Cleveland, Ohio was best known as the place where **Chef Boyardee** got his start! Now, "The Cleve" is the capitol of Rock n' Roll in the USA (don't tell Detroit I said that)!

Hong Kong, China is where **East** meets **West**. Modern sky-scrapers are planned using the ancient art of **feng-shui.** Feng-shui is arranging things in such a way as to make you feel good. Like how I keep my **peas** completely seperate from my **mashed potatoes** on my plate. Otherwise it doesn't feel right. Do you ever arrange your toys until they look "just right?"

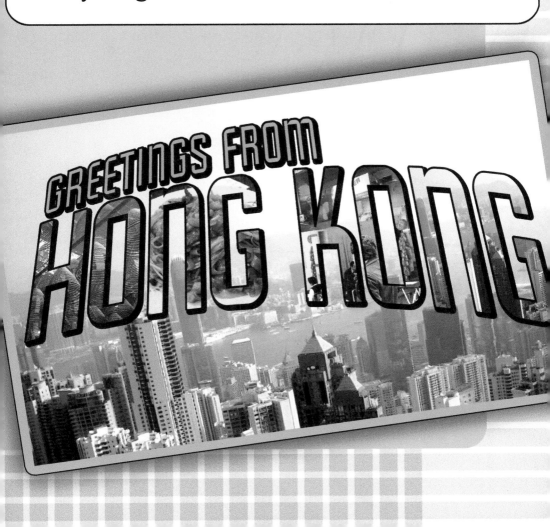

GREETINGS FROM HONG KONG

London, England is a very swinging place! There's a **queen** and the famous **London Bridge** and the great-grand-father clock "**Big Ben**." Also, a lot of rain and really good Indian food!

Rome, Italy is a city like no other! There are ancient monuments everywhere you look! The largest is The Colliseum. A long-time ago, gladiators fought each-other here for the entertainment of the Roman people. They also displayed exotic wild animals. The first giraffes, elephants, rhinos and crocodiles ever seen in Europe were put on display here. What a zoo!

Fun Fact: Romans were masters of road-building, but definitely not city planning. Most people think a map of Rome's streets looks like a plate of spaghetti!

Prague is the capitol city of the **Czech Republic**. It's got amazing architecture! Here, you'll find palaces, towers, a castle and **labyrinth**.

Fun Fact: Prague is a great city for kids! They have a huge Toy Museum, and a Museum for Children's Drawings. I wonder how many refrigerators and magnets they need to display all that artwork? Is your fridge at home a **Museum for Children's Drawings?**

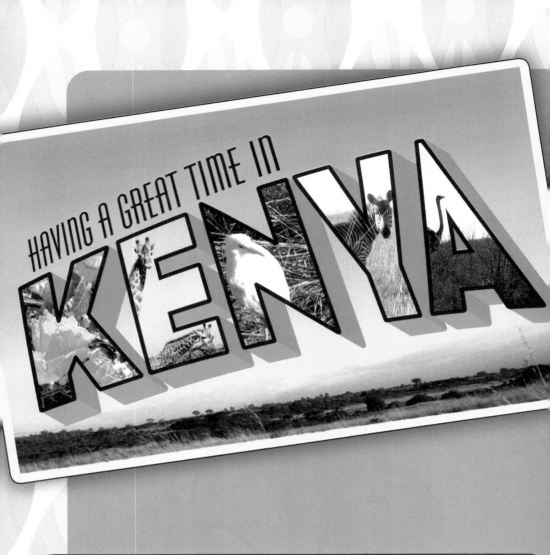

Kenya is a beautiful nation! It's home to some of the largest wild-life preserves on earth. They have so many different types of animals, you wouldn't find in any of the other cities we've explored: the aardwolf, bush babies, impalas, giant rats and the spectacled elephant shrews, just to name a few real (but made-up sounding) examples. What do you think an **aardwolf** sounds like?

Mexico City is the capital, and largest city of Mexico. This is the center of Mexican professional-wrestling called **LUCHA LIBRE!** It's one of the most popular sports to watch from Olympus! My favorite match is a "**Mask versus Mask.**" The loser is unmasked and his real identity revealed! These guys are like **super heroes**!

WE'RE SOUTH OF THE BORDER IN MEXICO CITY

Paris, France is the best place for food, art and seeing the **Eiffel Tower** or Lance Armstrong. Here you can visit the famous painting, **Mona Lisa**. I was there when Leonardo painted her: at first she was giving a big grin! I told Mona to take it down a notch, and the rest is history!

Fun Fact: The **beret**--a hat that looks like the top of an acorn--is popular in Paris with artists and students. It looks too awesome to only be worn in Paris though: did you know police in Hong Kong, Poland and Italy wear them too?

Vancouver, British Columbia is a fantastic **coastal city**. The Canadians are huge sports fans, and the biggest sport is **hockey**. Vancouver is one of the only places where you can ski, golf and and go sailing--all in one day!

YOUR COMRADES WELCOME YOU TO LENINGRAD

In **St. Petersburg**, Russia (formerly Leningrad) they really know how to appreciate the **fine arts**. Ballets and symphonies are regularly performed here. I like the **matroyshka dolls**--hidden inside each one are up to 10 more miniature dolls!

Sydney, Australia is a gorgeous place. They've got tons of great stuff--beaches, amusement parks, water-parks, go-cart tracks, an incredible **zoo**, and ice skating. Also, **The Wiggles**. Plus, people who live in Sydney are called **"Sydneysiders,"** which sounds pretty cool.

More people, super-heroes and super-villians live in New York, NY than any other city in The United States. There are more than **800 languages** spoken here--that's more than anywhere else on earth!

Fun Fact: New York has a ton of nick-names--not just "**The Big Apple.**" There's also: Gotham, Empire City, The City that Never Sleeps, The Capital of the World and The City So Nice, They Named it Twice. What's a good nick-name for your home-town?

PHOTOGRAPHS USED:

CLEVELAND flickr.com/photos/dougtone
HON KONG flickr.com/photos/dougtone
KENYA flickr.com/photos/irene2005
LENINGRAD flickr.com/photos/honzasoukup
LONDON flickr.com/photos/damo1977
MEXICO flickr.com/photos/22240293@N05
NEW YORK flickr.com/photos/29624656@N08
PARIS flickr.com/photos/gpalacios
PRAGUE flickr.com/photos/brighton
ROME/SYDNEY flickr.com/photos/eustaquio
VANCOUVER flickr.com/photos/gusilu